Dear Parent:

Congratulations! Your child is taking the first steps on an exciting journey. The destination? Independent reading!

STEP INTO READING® will help your child get there. The program offers books at five levels that accompany children from their first attempts at reading to reading success. Each step includes fun stories, fiction and nonfiction, and colorful art. There are also Step into Reading Sticker Books, Step into Reading Math Readers, Step into Reading Write-In Readers, Step into Reading Phonics Readers, and Step into Reading Phonics First Steps! Boxed Sets—a complete literacy program with something to interest every child.

Learning to Read, Step by Step!

Ready to Read   Preschool–Kindergarten
• big type and easy words • rhyme and rhythm • picture clues
For children who know the alphabet and are eager to begin reading.

Reading with Help   Preschool–Grade 1
• basic vocabulary • short sentences • simple stories
For children who recognize familiar words and sound out new words with help.

Reading on Your Own   Grades 1–3
• engaging characters • easy-to-follow plots • popular topics
For children who are ready to read on their own.

Reading Paragraphs   Grades 2–3
• challenging vocabulary • short paragraphs • exciting stories
For newly independent readers who read simple sentences with confidence.

Ready for Chapters   Grades 2–4
• chapters • longer paragraphs • full-color art
For children who want to take the plunge into chapter books but still like colorful pictures.

STEP INTO READING® is designed to give every child a successful reading experience. The grade levels are only guides. Children can progress through the steps at their own speed, developing confidence in their reading, no matter what their grade.

Remember, a lifetime love of reading starts with a single step!

Story
Collection

www.stepintoreading.com
www.barbie.com

Educators and librarians, for a variety of teaching tools, visit us at
www.randomhouse.com/teachers

ISBN-13: 978-0-375-84124-8
ISBN-10: 0-375-84124-5

Printed in the United States of America   10 9 8 7 6 5 4

STEP INTO READING®

Barbie™
Story Collection

Step 1 and Step 2 Books
A Collection of Six Early Readers

Random House 🏠 New York

Contents

STEP INTO READING®

STEP 1

Barbie™

A Dress-Up Day

by Jessie Parker

illustrated by S.I. International

Rain, rain,
go away.

"Hey! Let's have
a dress-up day!"

Open the trunk.

Look inside.

"Can I pretend
to be a bride?"

Try on Barbie's
beads and rings,

necklaces and

sparkly things.

A velvet vest.

A golden gown.

Kelly wears
a silver crown!

A purple scarf.

A pretty bow.

It is Kelly and Stacie's
Fashion Show!

Prance and dance
in Barbie's shoes.

Whirl and twirl
in pink tutus.

Barbie claps.

Take a bow.

"Do we have to
clean up now?"

No more rain.

Here comes the sun!

Dressing up was

so much fun!

Rain, rain,
what a day!
Come again
another day!

STEP INTO READING®

STEP 1

Barbie™

One Pink Shoe

by Salile Orr
illustrated by S.I. International

One, two.

One pink shoe!

Three, four.

Close the door.

Five, six.

Match or mix?

Seven, eight.

Don't be late!

Nine, ten.

Pick up Ken!

Barbie, Barbie,

you look great!

Are you ready

for our date?

Time goes by
way too fast.

But memories

will always last.

Ten, nine.

Wait in line!

Eight, seven.

Look! It's Kevin!

Six, five.

Splash and dive!

Four, three.

Look and see!

Two, one.

I have to run!

My one pink shoe!

It was with you.

Barbie™
School Days

by Apple Jordan
illustrated by Karen Wolcott

Time for school!

The clock is ringing.

The sun is up.

The birds are singing.

Stacie has a test today.

Kelly cannot
wait to play.

But first they have
so much to do.
They brush their teeth.
They wash up, too.

They make their beds.

They brush their hair.

Then they pick out
what to wear!

Barbie cooks eggs
for Stacie and Kelly.

For lunch they make
peanut butter and jelly.

They pack their bags
with things they need—
pens to write with
and books to read.

They button their coats.

They are on their way.

Everyone is ready for
a new school day!

The school bell rings.

They are not late.

"Good luck, Stacie.
You will do great!"

"So long, Kelly!
Go have fun.
See you when
the day is done."

Barbie rushes.

Hurry! Zoom!

Just on time

to her own classroom!

STEP INTO READING®

STEP 2

Barbie™

Two Princesses

by Bill Gordh

illustrated by S.I. International

It was a dark and stormy night.

Barbie was snug in her bed.

She could hear the thunder
outside her window.

In ran Kelly and Stacie.
"Thunder scares me,"
said Kelly.

"Tell us a story, Barbie,"
said Stacie.
"You make up the best stories."

Barbie looked around.

She saw a bunny.

She saw a big sparkly ring.

Bunny. Ring. Thunderstorm.

"Once upon a time,"
Barbie began,
"there were two princesses
named Kelly and Stacie . . ."

The two princesses
had magic rings.
The magic rings gave them
the power to talk to animals.

One day, the princesses
wanted to have a picnic
in the forest.

They filled a basket
with cheese, bread, carrots,
and nuts.

The two princesses
followed the river
to their picnic spot.

At last, they came
to Grand Oak, the biggest
tree in the forest.

The birds were chirping.

The bunnies were hopping about.

There was enough picnic food

for everyone!

Suddenly, the princesses
heard a loud rumble and crash.
Thunder!

They took their basket
and ran for cover
inside Grand Oak.

The rain stopped.

The princesses came out.

They looked around.

Where was everyone?

A bunny hopped by.

"Bunny, wait!" Kelly cried.

"Where are you going?"

Bunny said,
"I have nowhere to go.
My house is filled
with rain water."

Just then Bird flew down.

"Tweet, tweet!" cried Bird.

"It rained so hard,
  my nest fell out of the tree."

The two princesses looked at
each other.

They would help their friends.

"Bunny," said Kelly,
"we will help you dig
a new home."

Everyone went up the hill.
Stacie and Kelly dug
a nice new hole for Bunny.
"Thank you," said Bunny.

Kelly pointed to a tree.
"Bird," said Kelly,
"we will help you build
a new nest up there."

Everyone found twigs and
feathers and leaves.
They built a new nest.

Stacie climbed up the tree.

The nest was a good fit.

"Tweet, tweet!" said Bird.

"Thank you."

The two princesses
shared their picnic with
Bird and Bunny.

Stacie and Kelly smiled.
They loved helping
their friends.

Then it was time to go.
The princesses waved good-bye
and went back to their home.

"The end," said Barbie.

Kelly and Stacie looked up.

It was quiet outside.

"We like your story!" said Kelly.

"And now," said Barbie,
"the storm is over.
That means it is time for
all princesses to go to bed!"

Barbie™

Lost and Found

by Carol Pugliano-Martin
illustrated by S.I. International

Barbie was reading
in her room.
All of a sudden, she heard
Stacie calling from outside.

"Barbie! Come quick!"
cried Stacie.

Barbie ran outside.
"Look who followed me home,"
said Stacie.
"Can I keep her?"

Barbie knelt down
to pet the dog.
She let the dog lick her hand.

"I don't see a collar or a tag,"
Barbie said.

"Does that mean I *can* keep her?"
asked Stacie.

"Stacie, this dog might belong to someone. We have to find her owners," said Barbie.

"I guess you're right,"
said Stacie.

"Let's look for clues!"

"Well, she's all wet and muddy," said Barbie.

"Yes! That's the first clue!"
Stacie said.

She ran inside and got a notepad.

She wrote the clue on the pad.

"Now where could she have gotten so wet and muddy?" asked Barbie.

"There's a stream in the park,"
said Stacie.
They began walking.
The dog trotted beside them.

They came to the park.

The dog ran ahead.

"Barbie, she's heading right
to the stream," said Stacie.

When they got there,
the dog was standing
at the edge.
She was barking.

"This must be where
she got wet!" said Stacie.
"Do you like to swim, girl?"
The dog gave Stacie her paw.

"Look, Barbie," said Stacie.
"There's a branch in her fur.
It's another clue!"

Stacie wrote down the clue.
"Now we have to find
the bush it came from,"
she said.
They began to search the park.

"There it is!" cried Stacie.

They ran to the bush.

They saw something shiny.

It was a collar with a tag.

"The collar must have gotten

stuck here," said Barbie.

"Is your name Sophie?"

she asked the dog.

Sophie wagged her tail.

"The tag says Sophie
belongs to Mrs. Martin
on Oak Street," said Barbie.

They walked to the house.
Stacie rang the doorbell.

Mrs. Martin opened the door.

"Hi, I'm Stacie.

My sister, Barbie, and I think

we found your dog."

"She followed me home,"
said Stacie.
"I found clues and
we brought her here."

"Thank you!" said Mrs. Martin.
"You should be a detective
when you grow up.
You would be a great one!"

"I would like to work
at an animal shelter instead.
I want to help animals
find homes," said Stacie.

"Well, you're off to a good start!" said Mrs. Martin.

"Woof!" Sophie agreed.

Barbie™

A Day at the Fair

by Carol Pugliano-Martin
illustrated by S.I. International

It was a big day!
Barbie was
already dressed.
But Kelly was
still in bed.

"Time to get up!"
said Barbie.
"We are going
to the fair!"

Kelly jumped out of bed.

"Oh, boy!" she said.

"I will ride

the Ferris wheel

all by myself!"

Barbie helped Kelly
get dressed.
"The Ferris wheel
is pretty big," she said.
"Maybe I should
ride it with you."

"No, thank you,"
said Kelly.
"I can ride by myself."

When they got
to the fair,
Kelly ran to
the Ferris wheel.

She looked up, up, up
at the Ferris wheel.
It was very big.
And *very* tall!

"Are you ready to ride the Ferris wheel?" asked Barbie.

"Not yet," said Kelly.

Kelly and Barbie
saw a lady
making cotton candy.
They each had a
fluffy pink cone.

"Are you ready to ride the Ferris wheel?" asked Barbie.

"Not yet," said Kelly.

Kelly and Barbie
went inside
the animal tent.
Kelly oinked at a pig.

She petted a cow.

She even fed hay

to a goat.

They went back outside.
"Are you ready to ride
the Ferris wheel?"
asked Barbie.
"Not yet," said Kelly.

Kelly went
on a pony ride.
She waved to Barbie.

"Are you ready to ride
the Ferris wheel now?"
asked Barbie.

"Not yet," said Kelly.

Kelly and Barbie watched
the Ferris wheel
go around and around.
The children
riding on it
were smiling.

"Kelly, do you want
me to ride with you?"
asked Barbie.
"Yes!" said Kelly.

She and Barbie got onto
the Ferris wheel.

At first,

Kelly felt afraid.

She shut her eyes.

Barbie held her close.

They went up, up, up.

At the top,
Kelly opened her eyes.
She had never been
so high up before!
She could see
the whole fair.
"Wow!" said Kelly.
"This is fun!"

The Ferris wheel
went down, down, down.
Soon the ride was over.
"I want to ride again!"
said Kelly.

And that is just what
Barbie and Kelly did.

If you know the alphabet and are ready to read, look for these Step into Reading books:

ALL BETTER
AS YOU WISH ✪
BAMBI'S HIDE-AND-SEEK ✪
BARBIE: A DRESS-UP DAY ✿
BARBIE: ON YOUR TOES ✿
BARBIE: ONE PINK SHOE ✿
BARBIE: SCHOOL DAYS ✿
BEAR HUGS
THE BERENSTAIN BEARS:
   BIG BEAR, SMALL BEAR
THE BERENSTAIN BEARS
   RIDE THE THUNDERBOLT
THE BERENSTAIN BEARS:
   WE LIKE KITES
BIG EGG
BOATS!
BUG STEW! ✪
CAKE CAKE CAKE PIE
CAT TRAPS
CINDERELLA'S COUNTDOWN
   TO THE BALL ✪
CITY CATS, COUNTRY CATS
COOKING WITH THE CAT
DANCING DINOS
DANCING DINOS GO TO SCHOOL
DUCKS IN MUCK
FLY, DUMBO, FLY! ✪
FRIENDS FOR A PRINCESS ✪
THE GREAT RACE ➤
HAPPY ALPHABET ◆
HOG AND DOG
HOP, HOP, HOP!

HOT DOG
I LIKE BUGS
I LIKE STARS
JACK AND JILL AND BIG DOG BILL ◆
JUNGLE FRIENDS ✪
JUST KEEP SWIMMING ✪
JUST LIKE ME ✪
THE LION AND THE MOUSE
ME TOO, WOODY ✪
MOUSE MAKES WORDS ◆
MOUSE'S HIDE-AND-SEEK WORDS ◆
PIG PICNIC
PIGLET FEELS SMALL ✪
POOH'S CHRISTMAS SLED RIDE ✪
THE PUP SPEAKS UP ◆
SAMMY'S BUMPY RIDE
SLEEPY DOG
THE SNOWBALL
THE SNOWMAN
SUNSHINE, MOONSHINE
TAE KWON DO!
THERE IS A TOWN
THOMAS AND PERCY AND
   THE DRAGON ➤
THOMAS COMES
   TO BREAKFAST ➤ ✎
THOMAS GOES FISHING ➤
TOO MANY DOGS
WATCH YOUR STEP, MR. RABBIT!
WHAT IS A PRINCESS? ✪
WHEELS!

✿ A Barbie Reader
✪ A Disney Reader
◆ A Phonics Reader

➤ A Thomas the Tank Engine Reader
✎ A Write-In Reader

STEP INTO READING® STEP 2

If you can recognize familiar words and sound out new words with help, look for these Step into Reading books:

ALL STUCK UP
BARBIE: A DAY AT THE FAIR ✿
BARBIE: LOST AND FOUND ✿
BARBIE: ON THE ROAD ✿ ✎
BARBIE: TWO PRINCESSES ✿
BEARS ARE CURIOUS
BEAR'S BIG IDEAS ✎
BEEF STEW
THE BERENSTAIN BEARS
   BY THE SEA
THE BERENSTAIN BEARS
   CATCH THE BUS
BEST DAD IN THE SEA ✪
BONES
BUZZ'S BACKPACK ADVENTURE ✪
CAT AT BAT
CAT ON THE MAT
COUNTING SHEEP ✧
DAVID AND THE GIANT
DINOSAUR BABIES
A DOLLAR FOR PENNY ✧
A DREAM FOR A PRINCESS ✪
FIVE SILLY FISHERMEN ✧
GO, STITCH, GO! ✪
HAPPY BIRTHDAY, THOMAS! ➤
HENRY'S BAD DAY ➤
HERE COMES SILENT E! ◆
HOME, STINKY HOME ✪
HONEYBEES
I LOVE YOU, MAMA ✪
IS IT HANUKKAH YET?
JAMES GOES BUZZ, BUZZ ➤
LITTLE CRITTER SLEEPS OVER
MICE ARE NICE
MOUSE MAKES MAGIC ◆

MY LOOSE TOOTH
MY NEW BOY
NO MAIL FOR MITCHELL
OH MY, PUMPKIN PIE!
ONE HUNDRED SHOES ✧
PEANUT
A PET FOR A PRINCESS ✪
PINOCCHIO'S NOSE GROWS ✪
P. J. FUNNYBUNNY CAMPS OUT
P. J. FUNNYBUNNY'S BAG OF TRICKS
PLATYPUS!
A PONY FOR A PRINCESS ✪
POOH'S EASTER EGG HUNT ✪
POOH'S HALLOWEEN PUMPKIN ✪
POOH'S HONEY TREE ✪
POOH'S VALENTINE ✪
QUICK, QUACK, QUICK!
READY? SET. RAYMOND!
RICHARD SCARRY'S PIE RATS AHOY!
RICHARD SCARRY'S
   THE WORST HELPER EVER
SEALED WITH A KISS ✪
SILLY SARA ◆
SIR SMALL AND THE DRAGONFLY
SIR SMALL AND THE SEA MONSTER
THE STATUE OF LIBERTY
SURPRISE FOR A PRINCESS ✪
THE TEENY TINY WOMAN
THOMAS AND THE SCHOOL TRIP ➤
TIGER IS A SCAREDY CAT
TOAD ON THE ROAD
TWO FINE LADIES: TEA FOR THREE
WAKE UP, SUN!
WHISKERS
WHOSE FEET?

✿ A Barbie Reader
✪ A Disney Reader
✧ A Math Reader

◆ A Phonics Reader
➤ A Thomas the Tank Engine Reader
✎ A Write-In Reader